SISKIYOU COUNTY LIBRARY

D0871321

MY CAKE

mi pastel

BeanSprout BOOKS

ISBN: 1-7322049-1-8
ISBN-13: 978-1-7322049-1-1

PRINTED IN USA

Based on a true story

Basado en una historia real

Yo corto mi pastel.

I LIKE KETCHUP ON MY CHICKEN

Me gusta el catsup sobre mi pollo.

I EAT CHEESEBURGERS WHEN I DRIVE
Yo como hamburguesas con queso cuando conduzco.

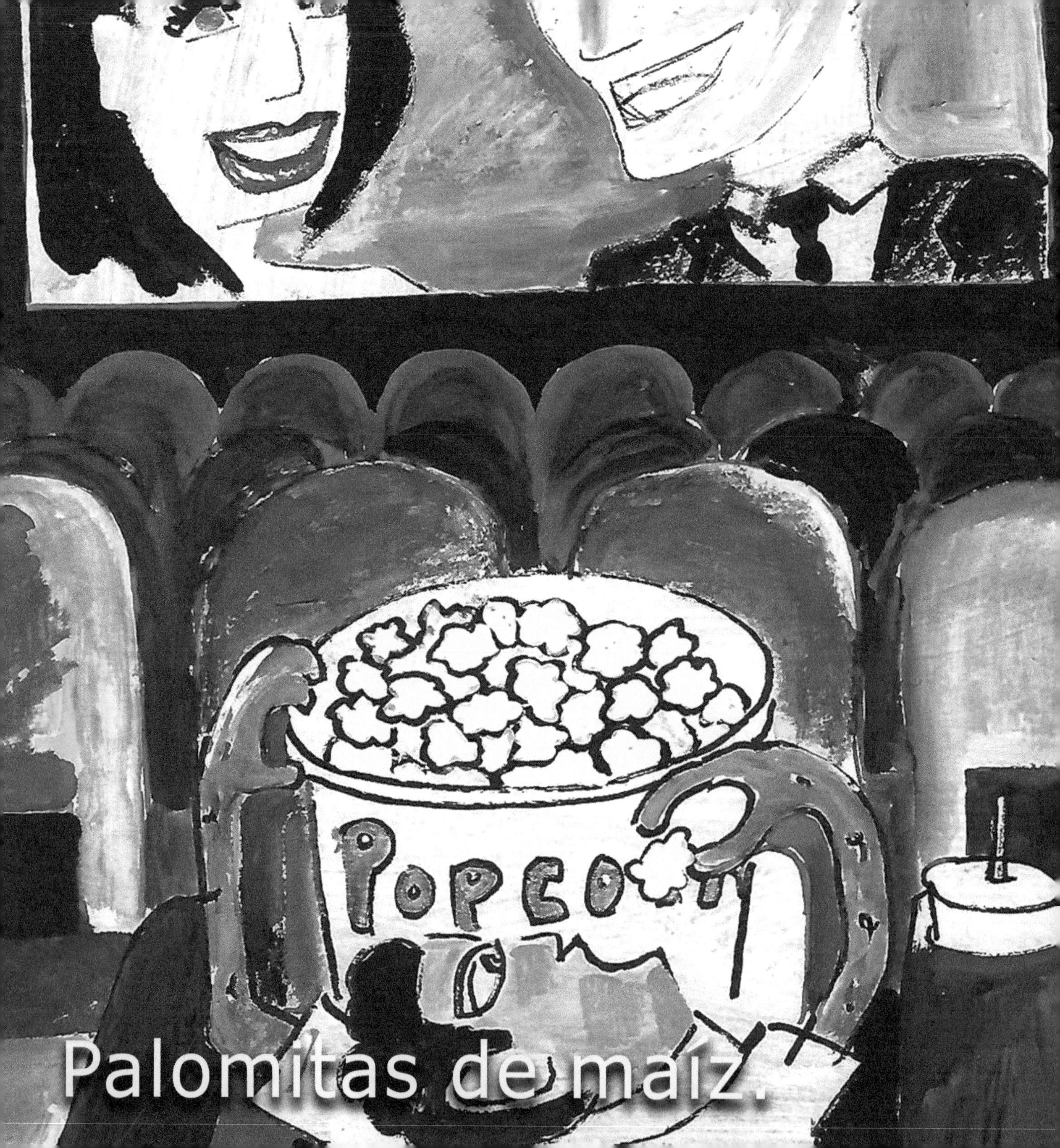

Palomitas de maíz.

I drink soda with the lights off.

Yo bebo soda con las luces apagadas.

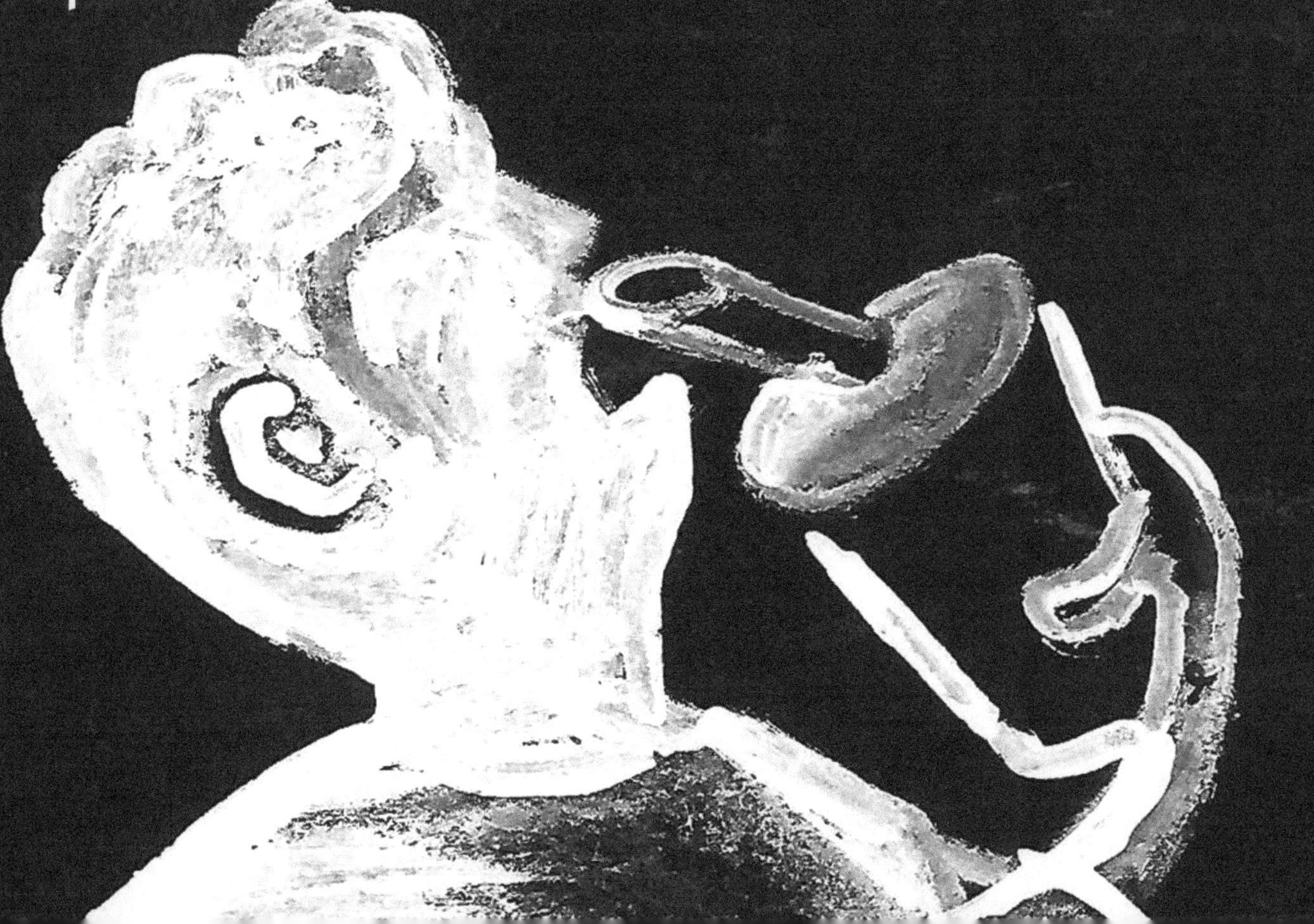

I chew my Smoothie.

Yo mastico mi batido.

¡Mantequilla de cacahuate y jalea!

I burn my steak.

50¢
AVOCADOS
make me Smile.

Aguacates de cincuenta centavos me hacen sonreir.

I crunch tacos sideways.
Yo crujo tacos de lado.

Ice cream and cake

Helado y pastel.

The fridge light went out.

La luz del refrigerador no funciona.

I hold my hamburger upside down
Yo sostengo mi hamburguesa al revés.

I fry my fish whole.

Yo frío mi pescado entero.

I spice my curry.

Yo condimento mi curry.

PICKLES

Pepinillos

That's what she said!

¡Eso es lo que ella dijo!

I get my pizza delivered.

Yo obtengo mi pizza entregada.

Chopsticks please.

Palillos, por favor.

I BAKE

Fried chicken.

Yo horneo pollo frito.

Crunchy chicken livers.

Los hígados de pollo son crujientes.

Sardine bones are edible.

Cacahuates Hervidos

Boiled Peanuts

Yo pela mi plátano.
I peel my banana.

I half-boil eggs.

Yo hago los huevos suaves hervidos.

Kitchen light on.

La luz de la cocina encendida.

Kitchen light off.

La luz de la cocina apagada.

paid advertisement

(anuncio pagado)

www.goodnightthebook.com

I like my nachos with beef and

Me gustan mis nachos con carne de res y

CHEE E
Queso

I mash potatoes

Yo puré patatas

en mis eggrolls.

in my eggrolls.

I masala my dosa

Yo masala mi dosa

and eat durian on my birthday.

y como durian en mi cumpleaños.

I DUNK MY DONUT...

Yo mojo mi donut...

Throw satay on the barbie.

Ponga las brochetas de carne a la parrilla.

Drink ice water without ice.

Chocolate milk before
I say goodnight

Leche chocolatada antes yo digo buenas noches

and pancakes when I say Goodmorning.

y panqueques cuando yo digo buenos días.

Almuerzo

Lunchtime

Would you like hot sauce for your burrito?

¿Quieres salsa picante con tu burrito?

SOFÁ

PIZZA

You sopped up all the grease with the last piece.
Absorbiste toda la grasa con la última pieza.

El Fin

The End

Written by
Tahlonna Grant

Illustrated by
Leeron Morraes

Graphics assistant
Netali Chapple

para mi abuela

www.beansproutbooks.com

CPSIA information can be obtained
at www.ICGtesting.com
Printed in the USA
LVHW07*0314140818
586914LV00018B/129/P

9 781732 204911